PIRATE TALES

The Pirate Lord

Bloomsbury Education
An imprint of Bloomsbury Publishing Plc

50 Bedford Square
London
WC1B 3DP
UK

1385 Broadway
New York
NY 10018
USA

www.bloomsbury.com

BLOOMSBURY and the Diana logo are trademarks of Bloomsbury Publishing Plc

First published in Great Britain 2011
This paperback edition published in 2017

A catalogue record for this book is available from the British Library.

ISBN
PB: 978 1 4729 4193 0
epub: 978 1 4729 5238 7
epdf: 978 1 4729 5237 0

2 4 6 8 10 9 7 5 3 1

Typeset by Newgen Knowledge Works (P) Ltd., Chennai, India

Printed and bound in UK by CPI Group (UK) ltd, Croydon CR0 4YY

MIX
Paper from
responsible sources
FSC® C020471

This book is produced using paper that is made from wood grown in managed, sustainable forests.
It is natural, renewable and recyclable. The logging and manufacturing processes conform to the
environmental regulations of the country of origin.

To find out more about our authors and books visit www.bloomsbury.com. Here you will find extracts,
author interviews, details of forthcoming events and the option to sign up for our newsletters.

TERRY DEARY

PIRATE TALES
THE PIRATE LORD

Illustrated by Helen Flook

BLOOMSBURY EDUCATION
AN IMPRINT OF BLOOMSBURY

LONDON OXFORD NEW YORK NEW DELHI SYDNEY

CHAPTER ONE
MISTS AND MUTTON

Devon, 1587

Sit by the fire. Go on, you look as wet as a herring. When the mist rolls in off the sea, it goes through you like there's ice in your blood. Sit down. I'll fetch you a pot of my best ale.

There you are, Sir, you should warm through in no time. The maid will light a fire in your bedroom and it'll be like toast when you're ready to go up.

Yes, I'm the landlord of this tavern. I own it. It's the finest tavern in Cornwall and I sell the finest ale. The name's Tom, Sir, Tom Pennock.

I know what you're thinking. How does a rough fellow like me come

to own a tavern as fine as The Golden Hind? I'll get the maid to fetch you a bowl of the best lamb stew you ever tasted... not mutton, mind you... real lamb. And if you've a half hour to spare before bed, I'll tell you how I earned my money.

I made it at sea, Sir. And, no, I wasn't a pirate... well, not really. If I *was* a pirate, then so was the greatest man that ever sailed the seven seas.

You'll have heard of Francis Drake... *Sir* Francis Drake they call him now. But I knew him back in 1577 when he was just plain Captain Drake to us.

I was ten years old when I first saw him. I was a skinny little lad, no higher than the rail on a poop deck. But I ate too much.

"That lad eats too much," my father said. "He'll ruin us. Bread for breakfast, cheese for dinner and cheese for supper. Eat, eat, eat, that's all he ever does. He'll have to go!"

"Go, Father?" I said. "Go where?"

"To a master – you work and he feeds you. Then your mother and me will be able to feed ourselves. A couple of your sisters are already serving in great houses. It's time for you to go, my lad."

"I could work with an ostler, Father, looking after horses. I like horses."

"Ha!" my father jeered. "You'd end up eating them. No, there's a ship in town. The men at the inn said the captain's looking for crew."

That was the only time my mother ever spoke up for me. "If you spent less time in that inn, Father, drinking away our money, you'd have more to feed our little Tom."

Father just snorted. "He'll have to get a job some time. The sooner he starts, the sooner he'll make his fortune."

"Fortune, Father?" I asked. "Can a sailor make a fortune?"

"Any man can make a fortune if he puts his mind to it."

"So why haven't *you* made a fortune, Father?" I asked.

"Shut up, son, and get your sea-boots on. You're off to see the sea."

He laughed at his joke.

I didn't.

CHAPTER TWO
GOLD AND GOODBYES

I cried. I'm not ashamed to tell you, Sir, I cried like a baby. I stood on the deck of the ship, the *Pelican*, and I sniffled.

Men and boys lined up on the sun-warmed planks. Some joked, some chatted like magpies and some stood grim-faced and angry. I was the only one weeping.

Suddenly, a cabin door opened and I had my first sight of Francis Drake. He wasn't a tall man, but he strutted around like our backyard bantam cock, eyes fierce in a wind-burned face, chest puffed out and beard ruffled by the breeze. Everyone fell silent.

The captain walked along the line, greeting some men as old friends. "Welcome on board, Jed Trickett... I see you're back for another shot at the Spanish, George Archer? Ah, Edward Marston... troublemaker, shirker and drunkard. Get off my ship!"

The man called Marston cursed Drake, spat on the deck and rambled back along the gangplank. He was halfway across when he lurched to the left and fell into Plymouth harbour. Everyone laughed and even I dried my tears and smiled.

Captain Drake reached me and asked, "Who have we here?"

My father jabbed me with his finger.

"Tom Pennock... Sir," I said.

"And you want to serve our queen Elizabeth, do you, Tom?"

I didn't know what he meant. Father spoke up. "He's the hardest-working lad you'll ever meet, Captain. Take our Tom with you and he'll kill twenty Spaniards before breakfast and then swab the decks to clean up their blood."

Drake laughed. "Then he's the lad for me. I'll set you to work as a cabin boy – serving in the galley... you know what a galley is?"

"No, Sir."

"It's the kitchen where we cook the ship's food... and when we go into battle, you'll be a powder monkey," Drake explained.

"He's a monkey all right," Father laughed.

"A powder monkey fetches gunpowder from the store below deck for the gunners. It's hot work and you have to be fast on your feet. Think you can do it?"

I had no idea if I could do it or not, but I said, "Yes, Sir." I already knew I'd have walked into the mouth of a cannon for that great captain.

Drake nodded at my father. "He'll do. Take a golden sovereign from the ship's purser on the foredeck."

Father grinned and almost ran to the man with a chest of treasure. He hardly stopped to wave goodbye.

And that's how I came to serve with Captain Francis Drake. I was sold by my father for a piece of gold.

CHAPTER THREE
RICHES AND ROBIN

For weeks we saw nothing but sea. I found I was one of the lucky ones. As Drake's little fleet of ships ploughed across the Atlantic Ocean, I was never sick. Bit by bit, I learned my job and I learned what our voyage was all about – treasure.

After I served the evening meal, the men sat below deck to eat it.

"The Spanish found gold and silver in South America," Jed Trickett told me. "They have an army of men out there working in the mines. They dig out tons of the stuff."

"They must be rich," I said.

"Well, the king of Spain is rich. The mine work is hard, and hotter than Hell, they say. A lot of men die."

"Are we going to dig in the mines?" I gasped. "I don't want to die!"

"No, Tom lad. The Spanish won't let us anywhere near their land. Our queen Elizabeth has a much better idea. She waits until the Spanish dig out the gold and load it onto their galleons. Then she sends Captain Drake to rob the Spanish ships."

"And *that's* how we get rich?" I asked.

Trickett nodded. "Half the treasure goes to our queen and the sailors share the rest with Captain Drake."

I thought about this for a while. "So we're robbers? Pirates?" I asked. I was worried. Every Sunday, the priest warned us about stealing. God would punish us, he said.

Trickett laughed. "No, lad. We're privateers – in private business. Where do you think the Spanish get their gold?"

"From the mines?"

"They *steal* it, Tom. South America isn't their land. They make the natives into slaves. They force them to dig for the gold.

Then they send it back to Spain. We just punish the Spanish for being so wicked."

And I believed him. When he put it like that. I grinned. "We're like Robin Hood?"

"Exactly like Robin Hood, if Robin Hood had a ship."

We weren't pirates – we were Robin Hood's merry men. But there wasn't much to be merry about on that voyage.

CHAPTER FOUR
STORMS AND SKULLS

Before we reached South America, we lost a lot of men. Some were washed overboard in storms, or crushed when a mast fell on the deck. Some killed each other in fights, and one man was executed for trying to start a mutiny against Captain Drake. But most of them died of sickness.

So many men died, we didn't have enough to crew all the ships. We sank two of the fleet in the Atlantic and just three vessels sailed on.

After two months, we landed for supplies in the place the Spanish call the Land of

Silver – 'Argentina' in their language.

We went ashore to gather fruit that would keep away sickness, and fresh water.

"I can't see any silver," I told Jed Trickett. I looked across the bleak beach and all I could find were bones. Scattered skulls had been pecked clean by rats and seabirds.

Captain Drake walked beside me and picked up a skull. "A sailor called Magellan came this way a hundred years ago," he told me. "Some of his men refused to go on, so he had them executed."

"Why did they refuse?"

Drake stroked his beard, which was longer and wilder than it had been when we left Plymouth. "Because they knew what was coming." He leaned forward and glared at me. "We've seen storms in the Atlantic, lad, but they're nothing to what we face next. When we sail around the southern tip of America, the seas are taller than three ships. Bad sailors get their ships snapped like dry twigs."

I trembled. "But we're not bad sailors, Captain Drake."

"We'll soon find out," he snorted. "Are you scared?"

"Yes."

"Then we'll leave you here with the skeletons," he said and walked back to the supply boat.

I ran after him.

The seas were as rough as the captain promised. No one slept for three days as we fought to keep the ship heading into the waves. If we let the waves hit us on the side, we'd be broken into splinters.

Every day, someone seemed to go missing. Waves like mountains washed over the deck and anyone caught in the open was carried away with them.

Men worked with buckets to keep the *Pelican* afloat. I took them bread and cheese, but it was wet and salty by the time they pushed it into their mouths. They looked as ghastly as the skeletons on the beach in Argentina.

I huddled in the corner of the galley, exhausted, and waited to die.

Chapter Five
Salt and Sun

Jed Trickett shook me until I woke. His face was crusted with dry salt, his lips were cracked and bleeding, and I thought he was a ghost come to take me to heaven. The ship was rocking but no longer being tossed up and down like a child's rag ball.

"We're through the worst," Jed said.

"I'm not dead?" I asked.

"I don't think so," he chuckled. "Come on deck and look at the Pacific Ocean. Not many English people have done that."

The sun dazzled me as it glinted off the clear water. A few weary men hauled on ropes to raise the sails. We were alone.

"Where are the other ships?" I asked.

"Gone, lad, gone," Drake said. He looked as tired as any man and his eyes were hollow caves. "One went down in the night... we couldn't save a single soul. The other was too battered to go on. I sent her back to England."

"But we got through," Jed said with a sigh. "The *Pelican's* a lucky ship."

Drake nodded. "And I've decided to change her name – from now on we'll call her the *Golden Hind*."

"*Golden Hind*?" I said. I liked the name. "So do we have to sail the *Golden Hind* through all that again, Captain?" I asked. "Are we going to get back home the way we came?"

"No. The world is like a ball, you know. If we keep sailing west, we'll end up where we started."

"Is that where we're headed now?"

Drake managed a grin. "Not until we've done what we came to do."

"Rob the Spanish," Jed Trickett said and rubbed his hands.

Drake turned on him. "Eat some fruit, Trickett... those cracked lips tell me you're going down with scurvy. If you get any worse, you'll be too dead to enjoy it."

Jed nodded and headed for the galley where the ship's cook was trying to boil up some dried beef into a stew.

Captain Drake looked to the stern of the ship. "Steersman, head north. There are some Spaniards who can't wait to give us their gold."

The men gave a cheer. It was a weak, croaking cheer, but the storms had failed to crush the hope from our hearts.

Chapter Six
Pacific Plots

It took us a month to reach the place that had the greatest treasure. We stopped along the way and raided small Spanish ports. Drake collected better maps from them, but when we raided Mocha Island, all he got was a nasty wound from the natives.

I stayed on the ship when the crew went on the raids. I remember the day they carried Captain Drake back onto the ship with his cheek sliced open. George Archer sewed it up with sail thread, and the captain was back in charge the next day. He always carried the scar after that.

As we sailed north on the *Golden Hind*, Drake placed a finger on the map. "That's where we're headed for, lads. Valparaiso. The biggest Spanish port on this coast. And that means the biggest ships with the biggest haul of treasure."

We reached Valparaiso harbour three days later. A galleon was sitting at anchor in the harbour. Drake called his men onto the deck. "That's a Spanish treasure ship," he said. "Would anyone care to make himself a little richer?"

We laughed. Our mood was better already. Drake sent me up to the top of the mast to get a better look. "She only has a handful of men to guard her," I called down.

"Let's knock her masts down with shot so she can't escape," Jed said.

Drake stroked his beard and thought for a while. Finally, he said, "Trickett."

"Yes, Sir?"

"If you were a guard on that Spanish ship, what would you do if this ship came at you firing all guns?"

"Fire back, Sir."

"And if she fires back with those huge cannon, what might happen to your head if it was hit by a cannon ball?"

"It would bounce off!" someone called.

"Ah, but it might bounce onto the deck and smash the *Golden Hind*," Drake said. "Now, what would those Spanish think if we sailed close to her, said 'Hello' – in Spanish – and asked them to get some wine ready for us?"

The men looked uncertain.

Jed said, "They won't be expecting an English ship, that's for sure. The English have never sailed the Pacific, have they?"

It was a wild, mad plan that would never

work, I decided. But Drake's eyes were glowing with excitement. That's when he turned to me and said, "It's time we brought young Tom along on a raid. When they see a little cabin boy, they'll never guess we plan to rob them. Are you ready to make your fortune, Tom?" he asked.

No! my heart screamed. But "Yes" was the word that came out of my mouth.

CHAPTER SEVEN
LADDERS AND LANTERNS

The plan was formed quickly and by the time we reached the Spanish galleon we all knew our parts.

The galleon looked like a floating castle. Black cannon gaped at us open-mouthed, ready to spit death at our small ship.

Jed Trickett led the way. "*Buenas tardes, encantado*," he called up the steep sides of the ship. "*Qué tal?*"

George Archer whispered to me. "That means, 'Hello, how are you?'" he explained.

The Spanish sailors lowered a rope ladder and Jed climbed up it. He jumped aboard the galleon and about ten of us followed him.

"*Amigo!*" the Spanish guard cried and opened his arms wide to greet Jed Trickett.

Jed Trickett punched him suddenly in the face. The man hit the deck with a clatter of his helmet. Our crew drew pistols and waved them. The Spanish guards turned, dived over the side and swam for the port.

No one tried to stop us as we searched the ship. I was the one who took a lantern down the narrow stairways. I was the powder monkey, quick and small enough to run below deck.

But the ship was like the maze old King Henry had made at Hampton Court Palace. I was soon lost and started to climb the ladders that led back up to the main deck. I ran back to where our crew waited. "Nothing," I said.

Jed looked over to the harbour, where the first escaping Spaniards were struggling onto the sea wall. "We have to be quick. They'll be back with muskets and gunships."

"We can sink them with their own cannon," I argued.

"There aren't enough of us to load and fire two cannon, even if we knew where they kept their powder and shot."

Suddenly, Drake hauled himself over the side of the ship. He stalked over to the groaning sailor who'd been knocked flat by Jed. "So, *amigo*. Where is the gold? Where is the treasure?"

The man looked up at Drake's scarred face and wild beard. "*Draco!*" he gasped.

That's what the Spanish call Drake, Sir, *Draco*... it means Dragon.

"That's right... *Draco*," he replied. "Come on your ship breathing fire. Now, tell me where you store the treasure. *El oro*?"

I could see now that the guard wasn't much older than me. He stumbled to his feet. "*Draco* is devil. I no give my king *oro* to devil!" he cried.

"Let's hang him from the mast," Captain Drake said wearily. "Pass me that rope."

"No, that's cruel!" I shouted. "He's too young to die."

Drake turned his dark eyes on me. "No one is too young to die. Not even you, Tom lad. If you want to argue with your captain, that is mutiny. And you know what happens to men who mutiny?"

"They get killed," I said.

"So? Do you want to hang alongside your Spanish friend? Or do you want me to cut off your head with my rusty old sword?"

CHAPTER EIGHT
NOOSE AND NECK

I tell you, Sir, I've faced a hundred freezing storms and laughed at them. But those words from Captain Drake turned me colder than an albatross's foot.

I don't remember what I said. "Don't cut off my head, Sir... and don't hang me... I didn't mean to argue, oh, spare me, Sir..."

Drake turned his back on my bubbling and babbling. "Put a rope around the Spanish lad's neck," he ordered.

Jed hurried to obey. The Spanish boy's olive skin turned pale green with terror as a noose slipped over his neck.

Captain Drake jerked on the end of the rope. "The gold... *oro*... where is the *oro*, lad?"

The boy just shook his head.

Drake shrugged and dragged the Spaniard up the stairs onto the rear deck. It was a drop of six foot onto the main deck. He threw one end of the rope over the spar of the mizzenmast. "*Oro*... or die... *quieres morir?*" the captain asked as he pushed the boy towards the rail. He picked him up and sat him on the rail till the Spaniard looked at the drop below him.

I looked at the end of the rope. Captain Drake hadn't tied it to anything. The boy didn't know that.

"*Oro?*" Drake asked.

The boy's mouth moved, but no words came out. Drake pushed him. The boy dropped the six feet to the deck and screamed. But the rope didn't stop him. He tumbled to the deck a sobbing, twitching jellyfish.

Drake walked slowly down the steps to where he lay. "*Oro?*"

"*En la parte trasera.*"

Drake nodded. "At the stern of the galleon, lads. We've been looking in the wrong place. Find it, Tom," he ordered.

I ran past the blubbering boy and through the ship's cabins. I was the one who found the twenty crates. They were too heavy to move and were bound with leather and iron so they were too strong to open.

Jed Trickett brought tools from the *Golden Hind* and after long minutes sweating in the stinking dark, we managed to open one.

Even in the weak light of the lanterns, the gold and silver bars were dazzling. No one was able to take his eyes off the magical metal. When Jed Trickett finally spoke it was in a whisper. "Let's get it back on the *Golden Hind*," he said.

As we hauled the first bucket up on deck, George Archer cried, "Spanish soldiers! The Spanish are sending their gunboats out from the harbour. If we don't move soon, we'll be dead meat."

Chapter Nine
Boats and Bullets

Drake gave his orders quickly and calmly. "The Spanish are coming from Valparaiso to the east. We'll unload to the west so the galleon shelters us. Jed Trickett... you hold them off."

Jed snorted. "By myself, Captain?"

"No, young Tom here will help you."

"Me?"

"Yes, you, Tom lad. Are you arguing again?"

"No, Captain," I said quickly.

"Take two muskets, powder and shot. Trickett will fire a musket while you load the other one. That'll give them something to think about. Now move, before I throw you to the fishes," he said.

We moved. We looked through one of the cannon ports and saw three gunboats heading towards us with about thirty soldiers in each. They were heading into the west wind, so they needed to be rowed by clumsy oarsmen. The boats were slow, but they would reach us before a quarter hour was gone.

Jed took the first musket and fired a shot that splashed harmlessly into the sea. "Missed," he muttered as I took the musket and passed him a loaded one.

Moments later twenty musket balls splintered the wood beside us. "They're good shots!" Jed laughed. "Better than me."

"The next round of shots could hit me!" I squawked.

Jed nodded. "That's one good reason for moving to another gun port," he said and crawled quickly along the deck to where another black cannon stood. "If I fire from here, they'll think we have quite a few musketeers... that'll slow them down."

I ran after him, keeping my head below the wooden rail.

Captain Drake was helping his men unload the treasure onto the boat. He watched it sail across to the *Golden Hind* and unload while our crew brought more onto the deck of the galleon.

"How are we doing, Trickett?" he asked.

"Keeping them guessing," he replied.

Drake shook his head. "This is too slow," he sighed. He called across the water with waving arms. "Bring the *Golden Hind* alongside – we'll load straight onto her."

Another round of musket fire smashed into the side of the ship. "I've been hit," Jed Trickett moaned, and fell backwards with blood streaming down his face.

The captain ran across to the deck. I thought he was going to help patch Jed's wound, but he didn't. No, that wasn't Drake's way. Instead, he pulled the wounded man away from the side and snatched up the musket. "It's you and me now, Tom, against the might of Spain. Keep loading."

"Yes, Sir," I said.

As my captain kept firing, I saw the Spanish boy begin to slip across the deck towards us. I'd just loaded a musket, and I pointed it at him. I'd never fired a gun in my young life, but I'd have shot him if he'd tried to harm my captain.

The boy shook his head and pointed at Jed, who was groaning and clutching at his face. "*Ayudará*," he said.

"*Ayud*... aid... aid him?"

The boy nodded. He tore at his shirt sleeve and made a bandage to stop the bleeding. If you ask me, he saved my friend's life.

But I was too busy loading muskets to worry about Jed just then. The Spanish gunboats were drawing nearer – the oarsmen clattering into the soldiers, who were standing up and trying to fire at us. I felt a shudder as the *Golden Hind* nudged into us. Loading the gold went much quicker. Our crew tipped the buckets down onto the *Golden Hind*, which was much smaller than the galleon.

At last the gunboats drew close enough for the Spanish to haul out their small cannon. Captain Drake and I watched as they loaded a stone cannonball and raised the barrel towards us.

Drake snorted. "They won't fire on one of their own galleons."

Three things happened very quickly. There was a puff of smoke and the stone ball flew towards us. The rail near our heads shattered into a thousand pieces. And, strangest of all, their cannon crashed backwards in the gunboat and sent Spanish soldiers tumbling, screaming into the water. The kick from the gun was so great it cracked the hull and we could see the gunboat start to fill with water. Soldiers scrambled to reach the other two gunboats, grabbed for the oars and almost upset them.

Drake laughed, rose to his feet and took off his hat. He waved it at the panicking Spanish. "*Adios, amigos...* from *Draco*!" he cried.

Then, to me, he said, "Time to go home, Tom lad."

CHAPTER TEN
WEALTH AND WOUNDS

We helped Jed down onto the *Golden Hind* and sailed off into the western sunset.

Captain Drake stood at the tiller that evening and said to me, "How does it feel to be a pirate, Tom Pennock?"

"Oh, but Captain Drake, I'm not! I'm a good citizen of England. I'm not a pirate."

"You are now, Tom," he said quietly. "You are now."

You know the rest, Sir. We sailed on robbing more Spanish ships of their gold and silver, spices and jewels. Then we headed west across the Pacific, past India and Africa, and home at last with a ship almost sinking with treasure.

The queen's share of the treasure was more than all the taxes she gathered that year. Captain Drake was a hero. Queen Elizabeth came aboard the *Golden Hind* in London and made him *Sir* Francis.

The queen was rich. But what about the English sailors? There were just 59 of us came home safe. We shared a quarter of the treasure 59 ways. More money than most men see in a lifetime.

But I'd had enough of the sea. I'd made so many friends and then lost them in the southern storms. All the money in Spain wouldn't bring my drowned friends back again. Jed Trickett knew how I felt. He said he wanted to buy an inn and settle down. I gave him my share of the treasure and between us we bought this place.

So how do I come to own it now, Sir? Ah, that wound on poor Jed's face never healed. Not really. He was always sickly after our raid on Valparaiso.

No sooner had we opened the inn, and changed its name to The Golden Hind, than Jed died. He had no wife or family.

The inn was all mine.

And that's the end of the story. I hope you enjoyed your lamb stew, Sir. It's been good serving you. Yes, I enjoy my life as a landlord. It's better than being a pirate, Sir.

When I was a pirate I was one of the 59 lucky ones. But you have to pay for your treasures, Sir. And a pirate pays in blood.

Aye, in blood.

EPILOGUE

In the story, Tom Pennock and Jed Trickett are made up – but Francis Drake and his famous voyage around the world are true enough.

Drake set off in November 1577. Only the *Pelican* made the trip through the storms at the southern tip of South America. After that, Drake changed her name to the *Golden Hind*.

He really did raid the port of Valparaiso by pretending to be friendly Spanish sailors, and he really did scare a Spanish sailor into telling him where the treasure was hidden by pretending to hang him.

Captain Drake returned home in September 1580 to be made a knight: Sir Francis Drake. The queen took a share of the treasure and that was his reward.

Queen Elizabeth wanted more, and sent off new fleets to rob the Spanish., This pirating upset the Spanish. In 1588 they put together a mighty navy – the Armada – and set off to conquer England. Drake was one of the captains of the little English navy that defeated the Armada and saved England.

Francis Drake was a thief and a pirate. He was also a great sailor and fearless fighter.

You Try

1. Drake's Drum

Drake's Drum is the snare drum that Sir Francis Drake took with him when he sailed around the world. Just before he died on his ship, he gave an order: the drum must be taken to his home, Buckland Abbey. Drake promised that if England were ever in danger, and someone were to beat the drum, he would return to fight for the country. The drum was kept at Buckland for many years. One legend said it could be heard beating at times when England was at war and in danger.

A poem called 'Drake's Drum' was

written in the 1800s. It is difficult to understand. Can you write a new poem about Drake's Drum, danger and how the ghost of Sir Francis saved the land?

2. Drake's flag

When Drake's small wooden ships sailed around the world, they were often blown away from each other in storms. If you spotted a ship a long way off, how would you know it was friendly? It could be a Spanish ship wanting to sink you! What Drake's ships needed was a special flag. Can you make that flag? Use colours, letters and numbers like "E I" (Elizabeth I) or some sign that means a lot to the English sailors – Drake's drum, maybe, or his sword.